*To Jacob, Olivia,
Nicholas, Sophie and Timothy*

First published in Great Britain in 1992
by Simon & Schuster Young Books

Photoset in 14pt Baskerville by Goodfellow & Egan Ltd, Cambridge
Colour origination by
Scantrans Pte Ltd

Printed and bound in Portugal

Simon & Schuster Young Books
Campus 400
Maylands Avenue
Hemel Hempstead HP2 7EZ

British Library Cataloguing in Publication Data available

ISBN 0 7500 1078 9
ISBN 0 7500 1079 7 (pbk)

Toby Forward

the Birthday Phone

Illustrated by Neil Reed

SIMON & SCHUSTER
YOUNG BOOKS

Chapter One

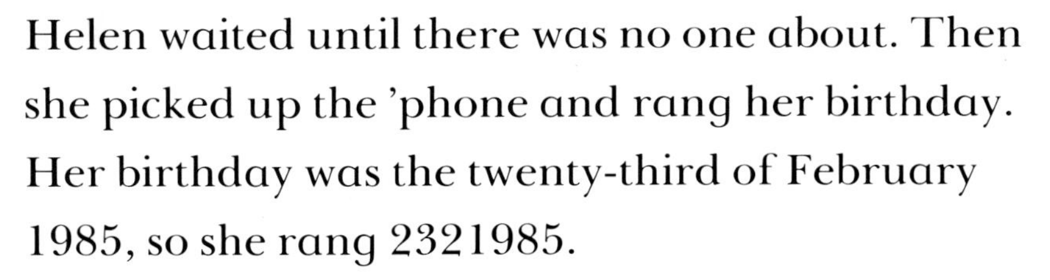

Helen waited until there was no one about. Then she picked up the 'phone and rang her birthday. Her birthday was the twenty-third of February 1985, so she rang 2321985.

Ring. Ring.

Ring. Ring.

"Hello."

It was a kind voice.

“Can I speak to the Birthday Fairy, please.”

“How did you know my number?” asked the kind voice.

“I rang my birthday,” explained Helen.

“Of course,” said the kind voice. “This is the Birthday Fairy speaking.”

“I’m very sorry about this,” said Helen, “but I don’t like my presents.”

"Oh dear," said the Birthday Fairy. "What did I bring you?"

"Don't you remember?" Helen was quite shocked. "It was only yesterday."

"There are a great many children," apologized the Birthday Fairy. "Such a lot to remember. And a lot of children have the same birthdays, of course."

"All right," said Helen. "Sorry."

"So, if you could let me know your name, and remind me of the presents."

"It's Helen," said Helen.

"Just a minute," said the Birthday Fairy. "I'll need to get a pencil and a piece of paper, and my glasses."

"You wear glasses?" said Helen in surprise.

"Magic glasses, of course," said the Birthday Fairy.

"Now," said the Birthday Fairy. "Dear me, that's made me quite out of breath. Now, are you ready?"

"Helen," said Helen. "And you brought me a new dress, some shoes, a pencil case and a doll. I like the doll," she added.

"And what did you want?" asked the Birthday Fairy.

"A water pistol, a big rubber spider, some itching powder and a bicycle," said Helen.

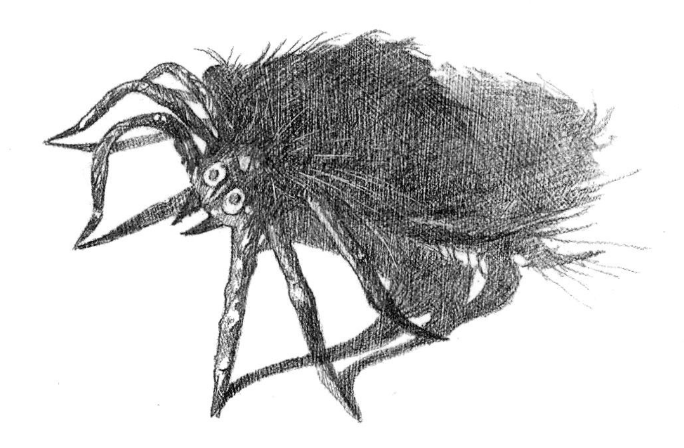

"I'll see what I can do," said the Birthday Fairy. "Please remind me of your address."

"You forget a lot of things don't you?" said Helen.

"There's such a lot to remember," said the Birthday Fairy. "Will you tell me?"

So Helen did.

Chapter Two

Two days later, the postman brought a parcel for Helen. It had a water pistol, a big rubber spider, some itching powder and a lovely card which said:

Sorry about the mistake.
I hope you like these. We do not have any bicycles at the moment.
love from
the Birthday Fairy

Helen did not tell her mum and dad about the itching powder.

They were very puzzled.

"Where did this come from?" asked her mum.

"The Birthday Fairy, of course," said Helen.

Helen's dad scratched his head. Then he scratched his shoulder. Then he scratched his leg. Then Helen's mum scratched herself.

"It's very rude to scratch," said Helen. And she smiled.

She told all her friends about the Birthday Fairy, but none of them believed her.

"That's silly," said Sally. "There's no such thing as a Birthday Fairy."

"It's your mum and dad," said James. "They give you all your presents. And your uncles and aunties and people like that. Only babies believe in fairies."

Helen pointed her water pistol at them and squirted.

The next year, Helen rang the Birthday Fairy *before* her birthday, to make sure.

"Hello, again," said the Birthday Fairy.

"I'm seven next Monday," said Helen. "And I want a real watch that tells the time, and a joke book, and I still want a bicycle, please."

"Leave it with me," said the Birthday Fairy. "I'll see what I can do."

On her birthday, Helen had a parcel from the Birthday Fairy with a real watch, and a joke book, and a box of stink bombs, but no bicycle.

"Where did these come from?" asked her dad.

"The Birthday Fairy, of course," said Helen. "Why did the boy swallow 25p?"

"I don't know?"

"It was his dinner money," said Helen.

"Uggh. What's that horrid smell?" asked her mum.

Chapter Three

James was very impressed with the stink bombs.

"I thought he was going to be sick," he said, as the teacher shooed them out of the classroom.

"Pooh," said Sally. "That was terrible."

"You are lucky," said James. "My mum and dad would never buy me anything like that."

"It was the Birthday Fairy," said Helen. "You don't think my mum and dad would buy them, do you?"

Helen's three friends looked at each other. It was a good point. Your mum and dad just didn't buy things like that.

"Tell us again," said James. "What do you do?"

"Just ring your birthday," explained Helen. "And you get your own Birthday Fairy."

"How did you know?" asked Sally. "Who told you about it."

Helen thought for a minute.

"No one," she said. "I just worked it out. How else would you speak to your Birthday Fairy? She isn't in the 'phone book, is she?"

They all laughed.

Sally rang up first. She used her very own birthday number.

Ring. Ring.

Ring. Ring.

"Brown's the Butcher," said a busy voice.

"Can I speak to the Birthday Fairy, please," said Sally.

"I can't hear you. Speak up."

This was not at all what Sally had expected.

"Is that the Birthday Fairy, please?" she said.

"What do you want? We're very busy."

"I want a doll's house, and a box of paints, and a slide for my hair, please."

"Name. Address."

Sally told him.

James looked in the 'phone book, just in case, before he rang his own birthday.

There was no number for the Birthday Fairy, so he rang his own birthday number. 1771985.

His Birthday Fairy was very busy and told him to get a move on.

James asked for a model 'plane, a pair of roller skates, and a big box of chocolates.

"It isn't my birthday just yet," he explained. "But I wanted to be sure you brought the right things."

"Birthday," shouted the man.

"Yes," said James, and he was so surprised at how loud the Birthday Fairy's voice was that he could hardly give him his name and address, but he managed it in the end.

The next day, Sally got a pound of sausages, a joint of beef, and a pork pie, and a bill for a lot of money.

James answered the door and there was a man with a box of groceries. He had a packet of corn flakes, a pound of butter, a tin of peas, a bottle of vinegar, and a big box of chocolates.

"And a birthday card," said the man. "We don't really sell those, and I had to go out and get it, special." And he gave James the box and asked him for a lot of money.

Chapter Four

They were all very angry with Helen.

"You tricked us," said James.

"My dad was furious," said Sally. "He had to pay for all those things. And we don't even eat meat."

"That's not what I call a Birthday Fairy," said James.

“Perhaps it’s because it isn’t your birthday yet,” said Helen. “Perhaps it only works on your birthday.”

“I told him that,” said James. ‘I said I’d wait till it was the right date.”

“It worked for me,” said Helen. “Really, it did.”

She was nervous when she rang her Birthday Fairy that afternoon.

Ring. Ring.

Ring. Ring.

There was no answer.

Perhaps you can only get through when it really is your birthday, thought Helen.

Ring. Ring.

Ring. Ring.

There was no one there.

Ring. Ring.

Ring. Ring.

Helen was just about to put the 'phone down when it was answered.

"Hello."

It was the Birthday Fairy's voice.

"Hello. This is Helen."

"Hello. Who's there?"

"This is Helen."

"Oh, dear," said the Birthday Fairy. "Oh, dear."

Helen thought she would put the 'phone down. She did not like this.

"I'm sorry," she said. "I'll ring you another time."

"No, please." said the Birthday Fairy. "Don't go." Her voice was different. It was sort of wobbly. "Who is it?" she said again.

"It's Helen. I know it isn't my birthday, but I wanted to speak to you."

"Oh, Helen," said the Birthday Fairy. And she sounded really pleased.

"Oh, it is good to hear you. I'm sorry if I was a little slow, I was asleep when you rang."

"Asleep?" said Helen.

"Yes. Silly, isn't it? Did you like the stink bombs?"

"Very much," said Helen.

"Good."

Helen told the Birthday Fairy how all the class had had to leave the room because the smell was so bad.

"Oh I am so pleased," said the Birthday Fairy.

Helen wanted to ask the Birthday Fairy about Sally and James but the Birthday Fairy started to say something else.

"Helen," she said.

"Yes?"

"Could you bring your dad or your mum to the telephone so that I can speak to them?"

"I don't want to," said Helen. "You're my Birthday Fairy."

"It would help me a lot," said the Birthday Fairy. "You see, I was asleep when you rang. And it was very good that you woke me up. Please could you get someone so that I can say what a good girl you've been."

"All right."

"Thank you."

Helen's dad was cross when she told him she had been using the 'phone.

"But it's the Birthday Fairy," explained Helen.

"Who is this?" he said when he spoke into it.

There was a silence.

"Oh," he said. "Yes. Yes, I see. I'll get a paper and a pencil. Can you hold on a moment? Good."

Chapter Five

As soon as he had finished speaking, Helen's dad ran out of the house. Helen was in bed when he got back home.

"We're going out," he said. "You were a good girl last night. How much have you got in your money box?"

Helen told him.

"That's more than enough." he said. "Bring it along."

They went to a flower shop and bought a bunch of flowers. Then they bought a card.

"We're going to see the Birthday Fairy," he said.

Helen was not quite sure about this.

"Do we have to?" she asked. "She's *my* Birthday Fairy. I don't want to share her."

"We'll see," said her dad.

"Where is she?" asked Helen.

"Strangely enough, she's in the hospital."

"Why?"

"She fell over last night and broke her leg."

"Can fairies fall over?"

"This one did."

"Oh."

"And she bumped her head."

Helen was sure this was wrong. Fairies don't bump their heads.

"She was asleep," said Helen.

"Sort of," agreed her dad. "At least, if you hadn't phoned she might never have woken up."

"Never?" said Helen in horror. "How do you know?"

"She told me her name and address yesterday and I went round there. I called out the ambulance and they took her to hospital. Here we are now."

And they were.

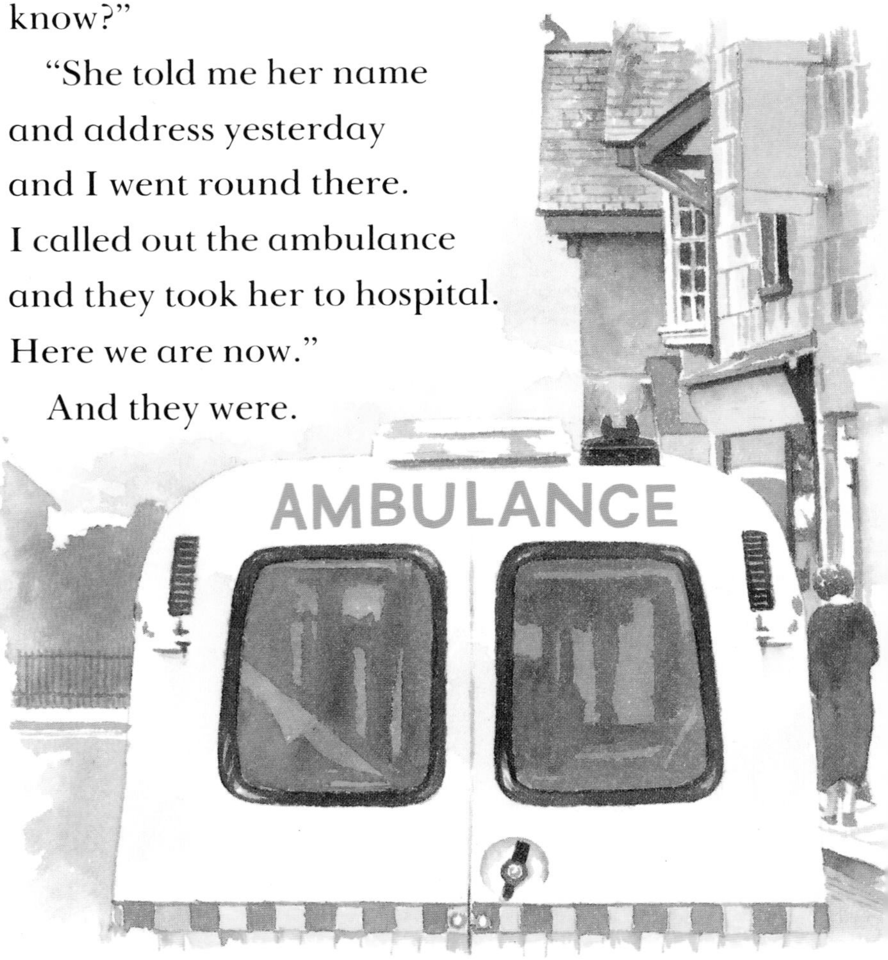

"And do you know," said Helen's dad, "it's her birthday tomorrow."

"Really?" said Helen.

"Really, truly," said her dad.

The hospital was huge. Helen thought she would get lost.

"It smells funny," said Helen.

"That's just Hospital," said her dad. "Mostly it just means things are very clean."

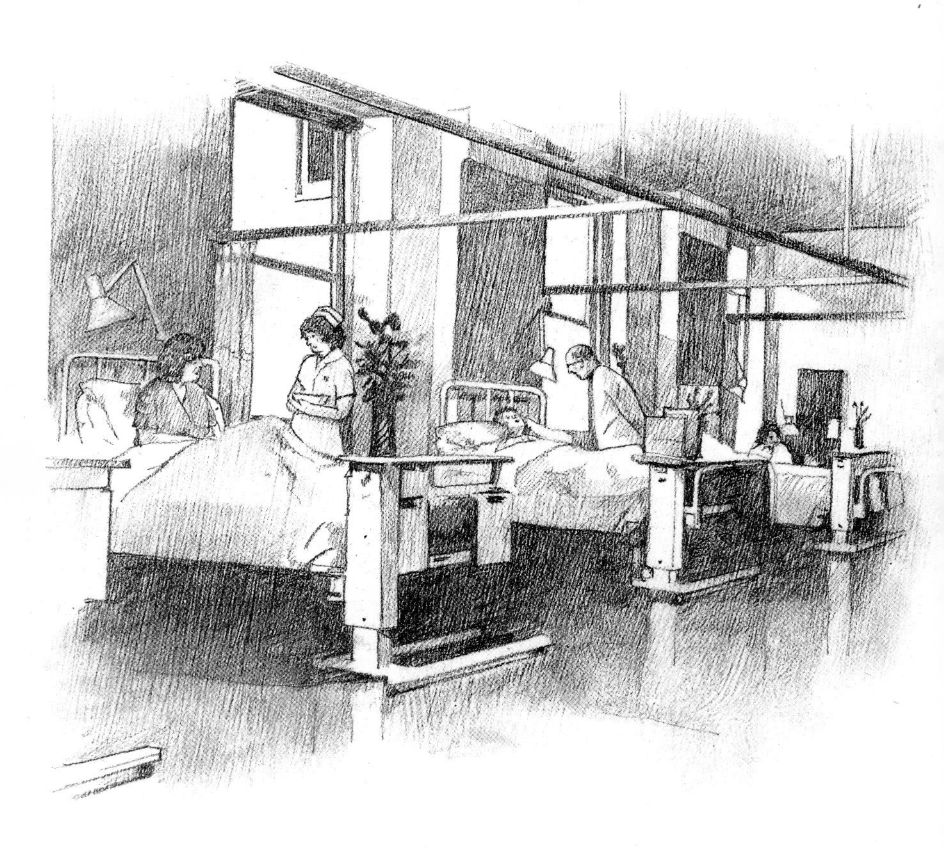

"Can we have a trolley?" asked Helen.

"I don't think so. It isn't a supermarket. Those are for people to ride on when they can't walk."

"I like it here," said Helen. "There's lots happening."

"It's a good place," agreed her dad. "This is her ward."

They walked in and saw rows and rows of beds.
Helen held her dad's hand.

"Which one is she?"

"Which one looks like a fairy?" he asked.

Helen looked. "None of them," she said.

"Come on. I'll show you."

Chapter Six

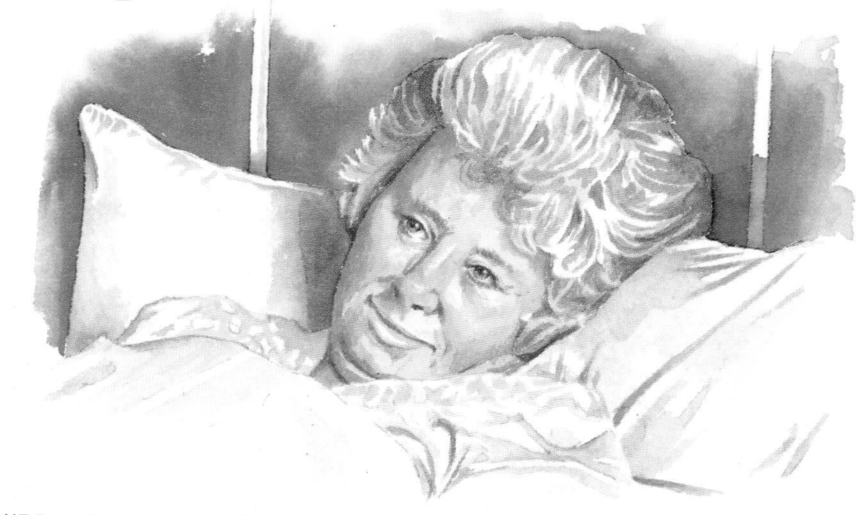

"You're very old," said Helen.

"Helen!" said her dad. "That's rude."

"Sorry," said Helen.

The lady laughed. She did look very old. Her hair was neat and tidy, but it was pure white. Her hands had small brown blotches on them. Her eyes were bright and clear, but the skin around them was netted with lines. And when she laughed her throat wobbled.

"I am though," she said. "I'm terribly old. And tomorrow I'll be a year older. Thanks to you, Helen."

Helen held out the flowers.

"These are for you," she said, "I bought them with my own money."

"Thank you so much," said the Birthday Fairy. "You are kind."

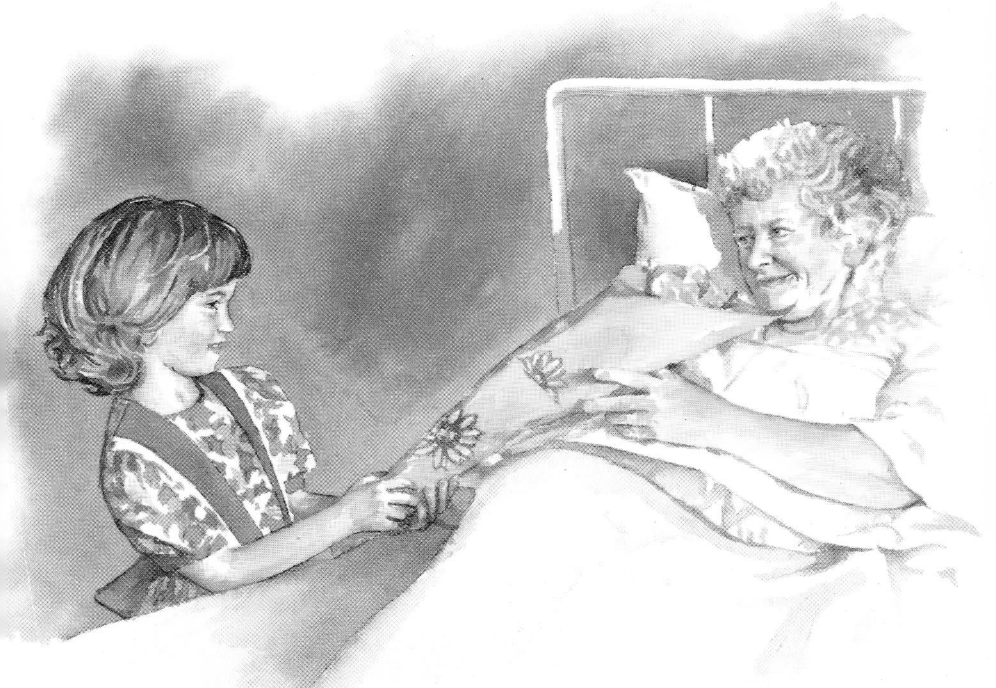

"Are you really the Birthday Fairy?" said Helen.

"I'm afraid not," said the lady. "I'm just an old lady."

"But you sent me the presents."

"I'm sorry about the bicycle. I couldn't afford that."

"That's all right," said Helen. "I don't mind. But you sent the itching powder and the stink bombs?"

"I'm afraid I did," said the lady. "I've always loved stink bombs."

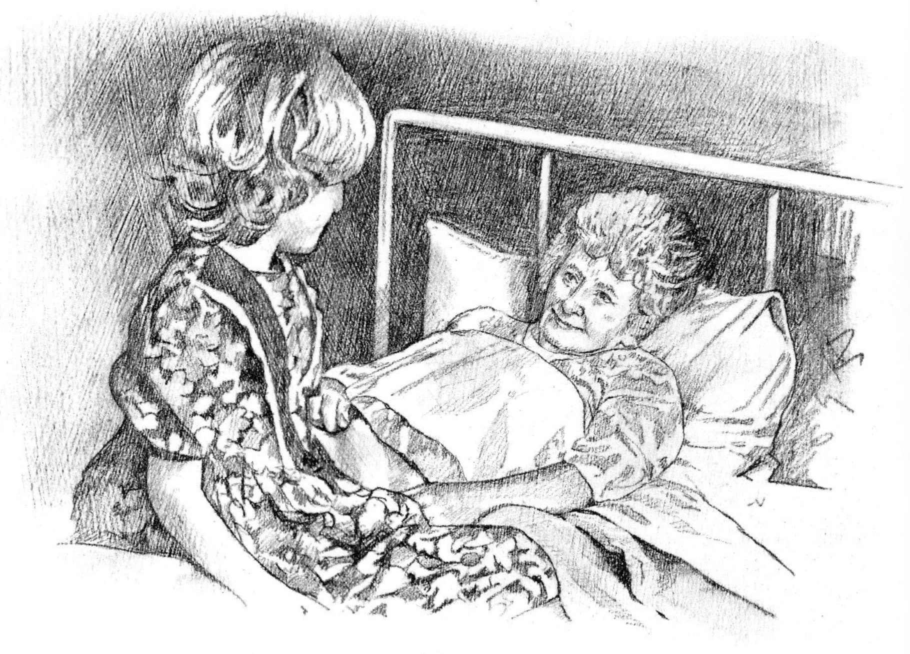

"You see," said the lady. "When you rang and asked for the Birthday Fairy I didn't want to disappoint you, so I played along with it."

"I'm glad," said Helen. "Is it really your birthday tomorrow?"

"It is. I shan't have much of one in here, but I'm glad to have one at all." She smiled. She had a lovely smile.

The next day, Helen and Sally and James and Helen's mum and dad sat round the lady's bed in the hospital ward.

"Oh, I don't know what to say," she said.

Sally and James told her about their 'phone calls.

"I do seem to have caused a lot of trouble," said the lady. But her eyes sparkled and she did not look at all sorry.

There were cups of lemonade and a plate of sandwiches and a plate of biscuits, and there was a cake and there were cups of tea for the grown ups.

“This is the best birthday I’ve had for years,” said the lady.

“We’ve brought you a present,” whispered Helen while her mum was pouring the tea and her dad was arranging the birthday cards on the cupboard. She slipped a little parcel into the lady’s hand.

“Stink bombs?” whispered the lady.

They nodded.

“Thank you. I’ll wait until you’ve gone before I use them,” she said.

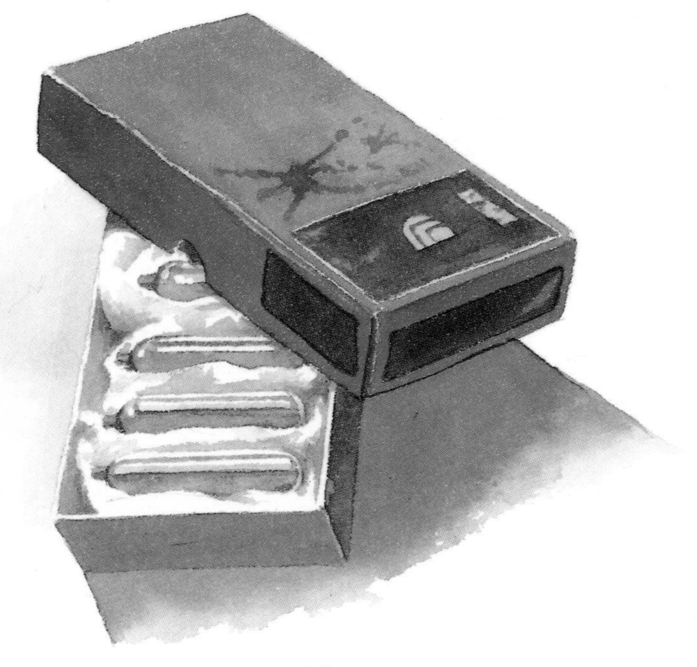

"Of course," said James, "I never believed in the Birthday Fairy."

"Neither did I," said Sally.

"But you all tried to 'phone her," said the lady.

The two friends looked shy.

"I do," said Helen. "I believe in the Birthday Fairy."

They raised their cups of lemonade and the grown ups raised their tea.

"The Birthday Fairy," said Helen's mum.

"The Birthday Fairy," they all replied. And they drank a toast and called out "Happy Birthday".

"The best birthday ever," said the Birthday Fairy.

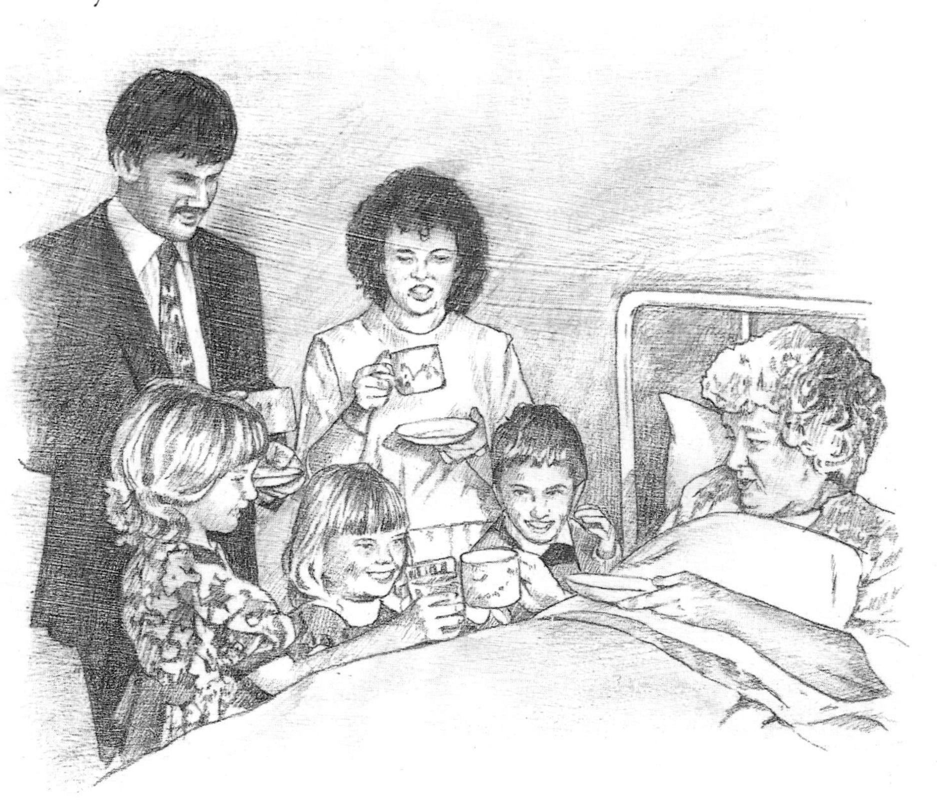

"Knock. Knock," said Helen.

"Who's there?" they shouted.

"Bert."

"Bert, who?"

"Birthday Fairy wins again," said Helen.

After the birthday tea they waved goodbye and left the lady. She smiled and waved back.

"I hope she'll be all right," said Helen.

"We'll come back soon," said her mum.

"She's so old," said Jack. "Will she be all right?"

"Oh," called a nurse. "What's that terrible smell?"

They looked at each other and laughed.

"She'll be all right," said Helen.

Look out for these other titles in the **Storybooks** series:

Look Out, Loch Ness Monster!
Keith Brumpton

For as long as he can remember, Kevin McAllister has longed to see the Loch Ness Monster. Then, one dark Scottish night, his dream comes true!

A Magic Birthday
Adele Geras
Illustrated by Adriano Gon

Maddy is delighted that Mr Osborne is going to do a conjuring trick at her birthday party. But she is very worried that there might not be a birthday cake . . .

Babybug
Catherine Storr
Illustrated by Fiona Dunbar

Tania's new baby brother has a baby alarm. "I wonder what people say about me when I'm in another room?" she wonders, and decides to change the baby alarm around.

Dreamy Daniel, Brainy Bert
Scoular Anderson

Daniel is always getting into trouble at school. But with the help of the brainy class mouse, Bert, Daniel learns to beat his day-dreaming habit.

Hopping Mad
Nick Warburton
Illustrated by Tony Blundell

Janey's little brother, Martin, is daft and completely useless. But he has one talent: he is very good at jumping around in a duvet cover. Janey has a wonderful idea – why not enter Martin for the big pillow race?

The Thing in the Sink
Frieda Hughes
Illustrated by Chris Riddell

Peter has always wanted a pet, but he never suspected that he would make friends with a long green slimy creature that lives in the bathroom basin!